George Savile Halifax

The Lady's New-Years Gift

Advice to a daughter - under these following heads, viz. religion, husband, house
and family, servants, behaviour and conversation, friendship, censure, vanity and
affectation, pride, diversion, dancing

George Savile Halifax

The Lady's New-Years Gift
Advice to a daughter - under these following heads, viz. religion, husband, house and family, servants, behaviour and conversation, friendship, censure, vanity and affectation, pride, diversion, dancing

ISBN/EAN: 9783337344580

Printed in Europe, USA, Canada, Australia, Japan

Cover: Foto ©Andreas Hilbeck / pixelio.de

More available books at **www.hansebooks.com**

THE
Lady's New-years Gift:

OR,

ADVICE
TO A
DAUGHTER,

Under these following Heads : *Viz.*

Religion,
Husband,
House and *Fa-*
mily.
Servants,
Behaviour and
Conversation,

Friendships,
Censure,
Vanity and
Affectation,
Pride.
Diversions,
Dancing.

The Third Edition Corrected by the Original.

London, Printed for *Matt. Gillyflower* in *Westminster-Hall,* and *James Partridge* at *Charing-Cross.* 1688.

LICENSED.

Jan. 9.
168⁷⁄.   Rob. Midgly.

ADVERTISEMENT.

THis Book being *ſent to a Scrive-*
ner to be Copied out, the Scri-
vener ſurreptitiouſly took another Co-
py of it for himſelf, and diſpoſing
it to a Perſon that knew not what
to do with it, and ignorant of its
worth, he ſold it us : We getting a
Licence for it, as a Book of an un-
known Author, put it to the Preſs ;
but finding ſuch a multitude of
Faults in it, as hath made us aſhamed
and troubled that ſo excellent a Piece
(according to the Univerſal Judg-
ment) ſhould be ſo mangled and abu-
ſed, we have made all the haſte we
could to get the Original Manuſcript
it ſelf, which the ſaid Perſon had,
and Printed this new Edition. The
Reader ſhall know this right Copy
from the other by the Engraved Fi-
gure before the Title.

Matthew Gillyflower.
James Partridge.

THE

Lady's New-Years Gift:

OR,

ADVICE

TO A

DAUGHTER.

INTRODUCTION.

Dear Daughter,

I Find, that even our moſt
pleaſing Thoughts will
be unquiet; they will be in
B   motion;

motion; and the *Mind* can have no reſt whilſt it is poſ-ſeſs'd by a darling Paſſion. *You* are at preſent the chief Object of my *Care*, as well as of my *Kindneſs*, which ſometimes throweth me into *Viſions* of your being happy in the World, that are better ſuited to my partial *Wiſhes*, than to my reaſonable *Hopes* for you. At other times, when my *Fears* prevail, I ſhrink as if I were ſtruck at the proſpect of *Danger*, to which a young Woman muſt be expos'd. By how much the more *Lively*, ſo much the more *Liable* you are to be hurt; as the fineſt Plants are ſooneſt nipped by the *Froſt.* Whilſt you are play-ing

ing full of Innocence, the
fpiteful World will bite, except you are guarded by
your *Caution*. Want of *Care*
therefore, my dear Child, is
never to be excus'd; fince, as
to this World, it hath the
fame effect as want of *Vertue*. Such an early fprouting
Wit requireth to be fo much
the more fheltred by fome
Rules, like fomething ftrew'd
on tender Flowers to pre-
ferve them from being bla-
fted. You muft take it well
to be prun'd by fo kind a
Hand as that of a *Father*.
There may be fome bitter-
nefs in meer Obedience : The
natural Love of *Liberty* may
help to make the Commands
of a Parent harder to go
B 2 down.

down. Some inward refi-
ftance there will be, where
Power and not *Choice* maketh us move; but when a
Father layeth afide his Authority, and perfuadeth only
by his Kindnefs, you will
never anfwer it to Good Nature, if it hath not weight
with you.

A great part of what is
faid in the following *Dif-
courfe* may be above the
prefent growth of your Underftanding; but that becoming every day taller, will in a
little time reach up to it, fo
as to make it eafie to you.
I am willing to begin with
you before your *Mind* is
quite form'd, that being the
time in which it is moft capable

pable of receiving a Colour
that will laft when it is mix'd
with it. Few things are well
learnt, but by early *Precepts* :
Thofe well infus'd, make
them *Natural* ; and we are
never fure of retaining what
is valuable, till by a continu-
al *Habit* we have made it a
Piece of us.

Whether my Skill can draw
the Picture of a fine Wo-
man, may be a Queftion ;
but it can be none, That I
have drawn that of a kind
Father : If you will take an
exact Copy, I will fo far pre-
fume upon my Workmanfhip,
as to undertake you fhall not
make an ill *Figure*, Give
me fo much Credit as to try,
nd I am fure that neither

B 3   your

your Wifhes nor mine fhall be difappointed.

RELIGION.

THe firft thing to be confidered, is *Religion*: It muft be the chief Object of your Thoughts, fince it would be a vain thing to direct your *Behaviour* in the World, and forget that which you are to have towards him who made it. In a ftrict fenfe, it is the only thing neceffary: you muft take it into your *Mind*, and thence throw it into your *Heart*, where you are to embrace it

fo

so close, as never to lose the *Possession* of it. But then it is necessary to distinguish between the Reality and the Pretence. *Religion* doth not consist in believing the Legend of the *Nursery*, where Children with their *Milk* are fed with the Tales of Witches, Hobgoblins, Prophecies, and Miracles. We suck in so greedily these early *Mistakes*, that our riper Understanding hath much ado to cleanse our *Minds* from this kind of *Trash*: The Stories are so entertaining, that we do not only believe them, but relate them; which makes the discovery of the *Truth* somewhat grievous, when it makes us lose such a Field

of

of Impertinence, where we might have diverted our felves, befides the fhame thrown upon us for having ever receiv'd them.   This is making the *World* a *Jeaft*, and imputing to God Almighty, That the Province he affigneth to the Devil, is to play at Blind-mans-buff, and fhew Tricks with Mankind; and is fo far from being *Religion*, that it is not *Senfe*, and hath right only to be call'd that kind of Devotion, of which, *Ignorance* is the undoubted *Mother*, without competition or difpute.   Thefe Miftakes are therefore to be left off with your Hanging-fleeves; and you ought to be as much out of counte-
nance

nance to be found with them about you, as to be seen playing with Babies, at an *Age* when other things are expected from you.

The next thing to be observ'd to you, is, That *Religion* doth as little consist in loud Answers and devout Convulsions at Church, or Praying in an extraordinary manner. Some Ladies are so extreme stirring at *Church*, one would swear the *Worm* in their *Conscience* made them so unquiet. Others will have such a Divided Face between a *Devout Goggle* and an *Inviting Glance*, that the unnatural Mixture maketh even their *best Looks* to be at that time *ridiculous*. These

af-

affected, Appearances are ever
suspected, like very strong
Perfumes, which are generally thought no very good
Symptoms in those that make
use of them. Let your ear-
nestness therefore be reserv'd
for your *Closet*, where you
may have God Almighty to
your self: In *Publick* be still
and calm, neither indecently
Careless, or *Affected* in the o-
ther Extream.

It is not true Devotion,
to put on an angry *Zeal*
against those who may be of
a differing Persuasion. *Partiality* to our selves makes us
often mistake it for a *Duty*,
to fall hard upon others
in that case ; and being
push'd on with *Self-conceit*,
we

we ftrike without mercy, believing that the *Wounds* we
give are *Meritorious*, and that
we are fighting God Al-
mighty's Quarrel ; when the
truth is, we are only fetting
out our felves. Our *Devoti-*
on too often breaketh out
into that *Shape* which moft
agreeth with our particular
Temper. The *Cholerick* grow
into a hardned Severity a-
gainft all who diflent from
them, fnatch at all the Texts
of Scripture that fuit with
their *Complexion* ; and becaufe
God's Wrath was fome time
kindled, they conclude, That
Anger is a Divine Vertue ;
and are fo far from imagin-
ing that their ill-natur'd *Zeal*
requireth an *Apology* , that
they

they value themſelves upon it,
& triumph in it. *Others,* whoſe
Nature is more Credulous than
ordinary, admit no Bounds or
Meaſures to it ; they grow as
proud of extending their
Faith, as Princes are of en-
larging their *Dominions* ; not
conſidering, that our *Faith,*
like our Stomach, is capable
of being over-charg'd ; and
that as the Laſt is deſtroy'd
by taking-in more than it
can digeſt, ſo our *Reaſon* may
be extinguiſh'd by oppreſſing
it with the weight of too
many ſtrange things ; eſpe-
cially if we are forbidden to
chew what we are command-
ed to ſwallow. The *Melan-
choly* and the *Sullen* are apt
to place a great part of their
Religion

Religion in Dejected and Ill-humour'd Looks, putting on an unſociable Face, and declaiming againſt the Innocent Entertainments of *Life*, with as much ſharpneſs as they could beſtow upon the greateſt *Crimes*. This generally is only a *Vizard*, there is ſeldom any thing real in it. No other thing is the better for being *Sowre*; and it would be hard that *Religion* ſhould be ſo, which is the beſt of things. In the mean time it may be ſaid with truth, That this *ſurly* kind of *Devotion* hath perhaps done little leſs hurt in the World, by frighting, than the moſt ſcandalous *Examples* have done by infecting it.

Having

Having told you, in thefe few Inftances, to which many more might have been added, what is not true *Religion* ; it is time to defcribe to you, what is fo. The ordinary *Definitions* are no more like it, than the common Sign-pofts are like the Princes they would reprefent ; the unskilful *Dawbers* in all Ages have generally laid on fuch ill *Colours*, and drawn fuch harfh *Lines*, that the Beauty of it is not eafily to be difcover'd : They have put in all the forbidding Features that can be thought of ; and in the firft place, have made it an irreconcileable Enemy to *Nature* ; when, in reality, they are not only *Friends*,

but

but *Twins*, born together at the fame time; and it is doing violence to them both, to go about to have them feparated. Nothing is fo kind and fo inviting as true and *unfophifticated Religion* : In ftead of impofing unneceffary Burdens upon our *Nature*, it eafeth us of the greater weight of our *Paffions* and *Miftakes* : In ftead of fubduing us with *Rigour*, it redeemeth us from the *Slavery* we are in too our felves, who are the moft fevere Mafters, whilft we are under the Ufurpation of our *Appetites* let loofe and unreftrain'd.

Religion is a chearful thing, fo far from being always at *Cuffs*

Cuffs with *Good Humour*, that it is inseparably united to it. Nothing unpleasant belongs to it, though the *Spiritual Cooks* have done their unskilful part to give an ill *Relish* to it. A wise Epicure would be *Religious* for the sake of *Pleasure* : Good Sense is the Foundation of both ; and he is a *Bungler* who aimeth at true *Luxury*, but where they are joyn'd.

Religion is exalted *Reason*, refin'd and sifted from the grosser parts of it : It dwelleth in the upper Region of the *Mind*, where there are no *Clouds* or *Mists* to darken or offend it : It is both the Foundation and the Crown of all Vertues : it is
Morality

Morality improv'd and rais'd
to its height, by being carried nearer *Heaven*, the
only place where Per-
fection refideth. It cleanfeth
the *Underftanding*, and brufh-
eth off the Earth that hang-
eth about our *Souls*. It doth
not want the *Hopes* and the
Terrors which are made ufe
of to fupport it ; neither
ought it to defcend to the
borrowing any Argument
out of it felf, fince there we
may find every thing that
fhould invite us. If we were
to be hired to *Religion*, it
is able to out-bid the corrupted World, with all it
can offer to us, being fo much
the *Richer* of the too in every
thing where *Reafon* is admitted

ted to be Judge of the Value. Since this is ſo, it is worth your pains to make *Religion* your choice, and not make uſe of it only as a *Refuge.*

There are Ladies, who finding by the too viſible decay of their good Looks, that they can ſhine no more by that *Light*, put on the *Varniſh* of an affected Devotion, to keep up ſome kind of Figure in the World ; they take Sanctuary in the *Church*, where they are purſued by growing *Contempt* , which will not be ſtopt, but followeth them to the *Altar*: ſuch late penitence is only a diſguiſe for the tormenting grief of being no more handſom.　That is the killing thought which draw-
eth

eth the fighs and tears, that appear outwardly to be applied to a better end.

There are many who have an *Aguifh Devotion*, Hot and Cold Fits, long Intermiffions, and violent Raptures ; this unevenneſs is by all means to be avoided : let your method be a fteady courſe of good *Life*, that may run like a fmooth Stream, and be a perpetual Spring to furniſh to the continued *Exerciſe* of *Vertue*. Your *Devotion* may be earneſt, but it muſt be unconſtrained ; and like other Duties, you muſt make it your *Pleaſure* too, or elſe it will have but very little efficacy. By this *Rule* you may beſt judge of your own Heart ;

Heart. Whilſt theſe *Duties* are *Joys*, it is an Evidence of their being ſincere ; but when they are a *Penance*, it is a ſign that your Nature maketh ſome reſiſtance ; and whilſt that laſteth, you can never be entirely ſecure of your ſelf.

If you are often unquiet, and too nearly touch'd by the croſs Accidents of *Life*, your *Devotion* is not of the right *Standard*, there is too much *Allay* in it. That which is right and unmixt, taketh away the *Sting* of every thing that would trouble you : It is like a healing *Balm*, that extinguſheth the ſharpneſs of the Blood ; ſo this ſoftneth and diſſolveth the *Anguiſh* of

the

the *Mind.* A devout *Mind*
hath this Privilege, of being
free from *Paſſion*, as ſome
Climates are from all manner
of venomous kind of Crea-
tures; it will raiſe you above
the little *Vexations* to which
others for want of it, will be
expos'd, and will bring you
to a *Temper*, not of ſtupid
Indifference, but of ſuch a
wiſe *Reſignation*, that you may
live in the *World*, ſo as it
may hang about you like a
looſe Garment, and not tied
too cloſe to you.

Take heed of running into
that common *Error*, of applying God's Judgments upon
particular Occaſions. Our
Weights and Meaſures are not
competent to make the Di-
ſtribution

ftribution either of his *Mercy* or his *Juſtice*: He hath thrown a Veil over theſe things, which makes it not only an *Imperti-nence*, but a kind of *Sacri-lege*, for us to give Sentence in them without his *Commiſ-ſion*.

As to your particular *Faith*, keep to the *Religion* that is grown up with you, both as it is the beſt in it ſelf, and that the reaſon of ſtaying in it upon that Ground is ſome-what ſtronger for your *Sex*, than it will perhaps be allow'd to be for ours ; in reſpect that the Voluminous Enqui-ries into the *Truth*, by Read-ing, are leſs expected from you. The *Beſt* of *Books* will be direction enough to you

not

not to change ; and whilst you are fix'd and sufficiently confirm'd in your own *Mind,* you'l do best to keep vain *Doubts* and *Scruples* at such a distance, that they may give you no disquiet. Let me recommend to you a Method of being rightly inform'd, which can never fail : it is in short this : Get *Understanding,* and practise *Vertue* ; and if you are so *Blessed* as to have these for your *Share,* it is not surer that there is a *God,* than it is, that by him all *Necessary Truths* will be revealed to you.

HUSBAND.

HUSBAND.

THAT which challen-
geth the next place in
your Thoughts, is, How to
live with a *Husband* : And
though that is fo large a Word,
that few *Rules* can be fix'd to
it which are unchangeable,
the *Methods* being as various
as the feveral *Tempers* of *Men*
to which they muft be fuited;
yet I cannot omit fome *General Obfervations*, which, with
the help of your own, may
the better direct you in the
part of your Life upon
which your *Happinefs* moft
dependeth.

It

It is one of the Difadvantages belonging to your *Sex*, that young Women are feldom permitted to make their own *Choice* ; their Friends Care and Experience are thought fafer Guides to them, than their own *Fancies* ; and their *Modefty* often forbiddeth them to refufe when their Parents recommend, though their *inward Confent* may not entirely go along with it : In this cafe there remaineth nothing for them to do, but to endeavour to make that eafie which falleth to their *Lot*, and by a wife ufe of every thing they may diflike in a *Husband* , turn that by degrees to be very fupportable,

C   which

which, if neglected, might in
time beget an *Averſion.*

You muſt firſt lay it down
for a Foundation in general,
That there is *Inequality* in the
Sexes, and that for the better Oeconomy of the World,
the *Men,* who were to be
the Law-givers, had the larger ſhare of *Reaſon* beſtow'd
upon them ; by which means
your Sex is the better pre-
par'd for the *Compliance* that is
neceſſary for the better perfor-
mance of thoſe *Duties* which
ſeem'd to be moſt properly
aſſign'd to it. This looks a
little uncourtly at the firſt
appearance ; but upon exa-
mination it will be found,
that *Nature* is ſo far from being unjuſt to you, that ſhe

is

is partial on your fide : She hath made you fuch large *Amends* by other Advantages, for the feeming *Injuftice* of the firft Diftribution, that the Right of Complaining is come over to our Sex ; you have it in your power not only to free your felves, but to fubdue your Mafters, and without violence throw both their *Natural* and *Legal Authority* at your Feet. We are made of differing *Tempers,* that our *Defects* might be mutually fupplied : Your *Sex* wanteth our *Reafon* for your *Conduct,* and our *Strength* for your *Protection :* Ours wanteth your *Gentlenefs* to foften, and to entertain us. The firft part of our Life is a good

deal

deal of it subjected to you in the *Nurſery*, where you Reign without Competition, and by that means have the advantage of giving the firſt *Impreſſions* ; afterwards you have ſtronger Influences, which, well manag'd, have more force in your behalf, than all our *Priviledges* and *Juriſdictions* can pretend to have againſt you. You have more ſtrength in your *Looks*, than we have in our *Laws* ; and more power by your *Tears*, than we have by our *Arguments*.

It is true, that the *Laws* of *Marriage*, run in a harſher ſtile towards your *Sex*. *Obey* is an ungentle word, and leſs eaſie to be digeſted, by making

king such an unkind distinction in the Words of Contract,
and so very unsuitable to
the excess of *Good Manners,*
that generally goes before it;
besides, the *universality* of
the Rule seemeth to be a
Grievance, and it appeareth
reasonable, that there might
be an *Exemption* for extraordinary Women, from ordinary Rules, to take away the
just Exception that lieth a-
gainst the false measure of
general Equality : it may be
alledged by the *Council* re-
tained by your Sex, as there
is in all other Laws, an Appeal
from the *Letter* to *Equity* in
Cases that require it, It is as
reasonable, that some *Court*
of a larger *Jurisdiction* might

be

be erected, where some Wives might resort and plead, *especially*, and in such Instances, where Nature is so kind, as to raise them above the *level* of their own Sex, that they might have *Relief,* and obtain a *Mitigation* in their own particular, of a Sentence which was given generally against *Woman-kind.*

The causes of *Separation* are now so very course, that few are *confident* enough to buy their *Liberty* at the price of having their Modesty so Exposed, and for *disparity of Minds,* which above all other things requireth a *Remedy,* the *Laws* have made no *provision*; so little refin'd are numbers of Men, by whom

whom they are compil'd. This, and a great deal more might be faid to give a colour to this Complaint ; but the Anfwer is, in fhort, That the *Inftitution* of *Marriage* is too facred to admit of a *Liberty* of *Objection* to it ; that the Suppofition of your being the weaker Sex, having without all doubt a good Foundation, maketh it reafonable to fubject it to the *Mafculine Dominion* ; that no *Rule* can be fo *perfect*, as not to admit fome *Exceptions* ; but the Law prefumeth there would be fo few found in this Cafe, who would have a fufficient Right to fuch a Privilege, that it is fafer fome *Injuftice* fhould be *conniv'd*

C 4. at.

at in a very few Inftances ,
than to break into an Efta-
blifhment , upon which the
Order of Humane Society
doth fo much depend. You
are therefore to make the beft
of what is *fetled* by *Law* and
Cuftom, and not vainly imagine, that it will be *changed*
for your fake. But that you
may not be difcouraged, as if
you lay under the weight of
an *incurable Grievance*, you are
to know, that by a *wife* and
dexterous Conduct, it will be
in your power to *relieve*
your felf from any thing that
looketh like a difadvantage
in it. For your better direction, I will give a hint of
the moft ordinary *Caufes* of
Diffatisfaction between Man,
and

and Wife, that you may be a-
ble by fuch a *Warning* to live fo
upon your *Guard*, that when
you fhall be married, you may
know how to *cure* your Husband's *Miftakes*, and to *prevent*
your own.

Firft then, you are to confider, you live in a time
which hath rendred fome
kind of Frailties fo habitual,
that they lay claim to large
Grains of *Allowance.* The
World in this is fomewhat
unequal, and our Sex feemeth to play the *Tyrant*, in diftinguifhing *partiality* for our
felves, by making that in
the utmoft degree *Criminal*
in the *Woman*, which in a
Man paffeth under a much
gentler *Cenfure.* The Root

and

and Excuse of this Injuftice
is the *Prefervation* of Families
from any Mixture that may
bring a Blemifh to them :
And whilft the *Point* of *Ho-*
nour continues to be fo plac'd,
it feems unavoidable to give
your *Sex* the greater fhare of
the Penalty. But if in this
it lieth under any *Difadvan-*
tage, you are more than re-
compens'd, by having the
Honour of *Families* in your
keeping. The Confideration
fo great a Truft muft give
you, maketh full amends;
and this Power the World
hath lodg'd in you, can hardly fail to reftrain the Severity of an *ill* Husband, and
to improve the Kindnefs and
Efteem of a *good* one. This
being

being fo, remember, That
next to the danger of *com-*
mitting the Fault your felf,
the greateft is that of *feeing* it
in your *Husband.* Do not
feem to look or hear that
way : If he is a Man of
Senfe, he will reclaim himfelf; the Folly of it, is of
it felf fufficient to cure him :
If he is not fo, he will be
provok'd, but not reform'd.
To expoftulate in thefe Cafes,
looketh like declaring War,
and preparing for Reprifals ;
which to a *thinking Husband*
would be a dangerous Re-
flexion. Befides, it is fo courfe
a Reafon which will be af-
fign'd for a Lady's too great
Warmth upon fuch an occa-
fion, that Modefty no lefs than
Pru-

Prudence ought to reftrain
her ; fince fuch an undecent
Complaint makes a Wife much
more ridiculous, than the In-
jury that provoketh her to
it.   But it is yet worfe, and
more unskilful, to *blaze* it
in the World, expecting it
fhould rife up in Arms to take
her part : Whereas fhe will
find, it can have no other
Effect, than that fhe will be
ferved up in all Companies,
as the *reigning Jeaft* at that
time ; and will continue to
be the common Entertain-
ment, till fhe is refcu'd by
fome *newer Folly* that cometh
upon the Stage, and driveth
her away from it.   The Impertinence of fuch Methods
is fo plain, that it doth not
deferve

deserve the Pains of being
laid open. Be assur'd, that
in these Cases your *Discretion*
and *Silence* will be the most
prevailing Reproof ; and an
affected Ignorance, which is seldom a *Vertue,* is a great one
here : And when your *Huf-*
band seeth how unwilling
you are to be uneasie, there
is no stronger Argument to
perswade him not to be unjust
to you. Besides, it will naturally make him more *yield-*
ing in other things : And whether it be to *cover* or *redeem*
his *Offence,* you may have the
good Effect of it whilst it
lasteth, and all that while
have the most reasonable
Ground that can be, of presu-
ming, such a Behaviour at
laft

laſt will intirely convert him.
There is nothing ſo glorious to
a *Wife*, as a Victory ſo gain'd :
A Man ſo reclaim'd, is for e-
ver after ſubjected to her *Vertue*; and her *bearing* for a
time, is more than rewarded
by a Triumph that will continue as long as her Life.

The next thing I will ſup-
poſe, is, That your *Husband*
may love *Wine* more than is
convenient. It will be grant-
ed, That though there are
Vices of a deeper dye, there
are none that have greater
Deformity than this, when
it is not reſtrain'd : But with
all this, the ſame Cuſtom
which is the more to be la-
mented for its being ſo general, ſhould make it leſs un-
eaſie

eafie to every one in particular who is to fuffer by the
Effects of-it : So that in the
firft place, it will be no new
thing if you fhould have a
Drunkard for your *Husband* ;
and there is by too frequent
Examples evidence enough,
that fuch a thing may happen,
and yet a *Wife* may live too
without being miferable.
Self-love dictateth aggravating
words to every thing we
feel ; *Ruine* and *Mifery* are
the Terms we apply to
whatever we do not like,
forgetting the Mixture allotted to us by the Condition of
Humane Life, by which it is
not intended we fhould be
quite exempt from trouble.
It is fair, if we can efcape
 fuch

such a Degree of it as would oppress us, and enjoy so much of the pleasant part as may lessen the ill taste of such things as are unwelcome to us. Every thing hath two Sides, and for our own ease we ought to direct our Thoughts to that which must be least liable to exception. To fall upon the *worst side* of a *Drunkard*, giveth so unpleasant a Prospect, that it is not possible to dwell upon it. Let us pass then to the more *favourable part*, as far as a *Wife* is concern'd in it. I am tempted to say (if the Irregularity of the Expression could in strictness be justified) That a *Wife* is to thank God her *Husband* hath
Faults.

Faults. Mark the seeming Paradox, my Dear, for your own Instruction, it being intended no further. A *Husband* without *Faults* is a dangerous Observer; he hath an Eye so piercing, and seeth every thing so plain, that it is expos'd to his full Censure; and though I will not doubt but that your *Vertue* will disappoint the sharpest Enquiries; yet few Women can bear the having all they say or do *represented* in the clear Glass of an Understanding without *Faults.* Nothing softneth the *Arrogance* of our *Nature,* like a Mixture of some *Frailties*; it is by them we are best told, that we must not strike too hard upon others, because we

our

our felves do fo often deferve Blows: They pull our
Rage by the Sleeve, and
whifper Gentlenefs to us in
our Cenfures, even when
they are rightly applied. The
Faults and *Paffions* of *Huf-
bands* bring them down to
you, and make them con-
tent to live upon lefs unequal Terms, than Faultlefs
Men would be willing to
ftoop to ; fo haughty is Mankind till humbled by com-
mon Weaknefſes and Defects,
which in our corrupted State
contribute more towards the
reconciling us to one another, than all the *Precepts*
of the *Philofophers* and *Di-
vines*; fo that where the
Errors of our *Nature* make
amends

amends for the *Difadvantages*
of yours, it is more your part
to make ufe of the *Benefits*,
than to quarrel at the *Fault*.

Thus in cafe a *drunken
Husband* fhould fall to your
fhare, if you will be *wife*
and *patient*, his *Wine* fhall
be of your fide ; it will
throw a *Veil* over your Miftakes, it will fet out and improve every thing you do,
that he is pleafed with. O-
thers will like him lefs, and
by that means he may per-
haps like you the more,
when after having dined too
well, he is received at home
without a *Storm*, or fo much
as a *repraachful Look*, the
Wine will naturally work
out all in Kindnefs, which
a *Wife*

a *Wife* muſt encourage, let
it be wrapped up in never
ſo much Impertinence : On
the other ſide, it would boil
up into *Rage*, if the miſtaken
Wife ſhould treat him roughly, like a certain thing called
a *kind Shrew*, than which the
World, with all its Plenty,
cannot ſhew a more Senceleſs,
Ill-bred, forbidding Creature. Conſider, that where
the Man will give ſuch frequent Intermiſſions of the
uſe of his *Reaſon*, the *Wife*
infenſibly getteth a Right of
Governing in the Vacancy,
and that raiſeth her *Character*
and *Credit* in the Family, to
a higher pitch than perhaps
could be done under a *ſo-
ber Husband*, who never putteth

teth himſelf into an Incapacity of holding the *Reins*. If theſe are not Intire *Conſolations*, at leaſt they are *Remedies* to ſome Degree : They cannot make *Drunkenneſs* a *Vertue*, nor a *Husband* given to it a *Felicity*; but you will do your ſelf no ill office in the endeavouring, by theſe means, to make the beſt of ſuch a *Lot*, in caſe it ſhould happen to be yours, and by the help of a wiſe Obſervation, to make that very ſupportable, which would otherwiſe be a *Load* that would oppreſs you.

The next Caſe I will put is, That your *Husband* may be *Cholerick* or *Ill-humour'd*. To this it may be ſaid, That
paſſionate

paſſionate Men generally make
amends at the Foot of the
Account : ſuch a Man, if he
is angry one day without
any *Senſe*, will the next day
be as kind without any *Reaſon* ; ſo that by marking how
the *Wheels* of ſuch a Mans
Head uſe to move, you may
eaſily bring over all his *Paſſions* to your Party ; in ſtead
of being ſtruck down by
his Thunder, you ſhall direct
it where and upon whom
you ſhall think it beſt applied.   Thus are the *ſtrongeſt
Poiſons* turn'd to the *beſt Remedies* ; but then there muſt
be *Art* in it, and a *skilful
Hand*, elſe the leaſt *bungling*
maketh it mortal.   There is
a great deal of nice Care required

quired to deal with a Man
of this Complexion; *Choler*
proceedeth from *Pride*, and
maketh a Man fo partial to
himfelf, that he fwelleth a-
gainft Contradiction, and
thinketh he is leffened if he
is oppofed; you muft in this
Cafe take heed of *increaſing
the Storm* by an *unwary Word,*
or *kindling the Fire* whilft
the Wind is in a Corner
which may blow it in your
Face : You are dextroufly
to yield every thing till he
beginneth to cool, and then
by flow degrees you may
rife and gain upon him :
Your *Gentlenefs* well timed,
will, like a Charm, difpel
his Anger ill placed; a *kind*
Smile will *reclaim*, when a
ſhrill

shrill pettish Answer would *provoke* him ; rather than fail upon such occasions, when other *Remedies* are too weak, a little *Flattery* may be admitted, which by being necessary, will cease to be Criminal : If *Ill-Humour* and *Sullenness*, and not open and sudden Heat is his Disease, there is a way of treating that too, so as to make it a Grievance to be endured : In order to it, you are first to know, that naturally *good Sence* hath a mixture of *surly* in't ; and there being so much folly in the World, and for the most part so triumphant, it giveth frequent Temptations to raise the Spleen of. Men who think right ; therefore that which

which may generally be call'd *Ill Humour*, is not always a Fault; it becometh one, when either it is wrong applyed, or that it is continued too long, when it is not fo : For this Reafon, you muft not too haftily fix an ill name upon that which may perhaps not deferve it; and though the Cafe fhould be, that your *Husband* might too fowrly refent any thing he difliketh, it may fo happen, that more Blame may belong to your *Miftake*, than to his *ill Humour*. If a *Husband* behaveth himfelf fometimes with an *Indifference* that a *Wife* may think offenfive, fhe is in the wrong to put the *worft fenfe* upon it,

D   if

if by any means it will admit a *better.* Some *Wives* will call it his *Humour,* if their Husbands *change* their *Style* from that which they ufed whilft they made their firft Addreffes to them : Others will allow no *intermiffion* or *abatement* in the Expreffions of Kindnefs to them, not enough diftinguifhing Times, and forgetting that it is impoffible for Men to keep themfelves up all their Lives to the height of fome *extravagant Moments.* A Man may at fome times be *lefs careful* in little things, without any cold or difobliging Reafons for it; as a *Wife* may be *too expecting* in fmaller matters, without drawing upon her-
felf

felf the Inference of being *unkind* : And if your *Huf-band* fhould be really *fullen,* and have fuch frequent Fits, as might take away the Ex-cufe of it, it concerneth you to have an Eye prepared to difcern the firft Appearances of Cloudy Weather, and to watch when the Fit goeth off, which feldom lafteth long if it is let alone; but whilft the Mind is fore, every thing galleth it, and that maketh it neceffary to let the *Black Humour* begin to fpend it felf, before you begin to come in and venture to un-dertake it.

If in the Lottery of the World you fhould draw a *Covetous Husband,* I confefs it

will

will not make you proud of your *good Luck*; yet even such a one may be endured too, though there are few Paſſions more untractable than that of *Avarice.* You muſt firſt take care that your *Definition* of *Avarice* may not be a Miſtake; you are to examine every Circumſtance of your *Husband's* Fortune, and weigh the Reaſon of every thing you expect from him before you have right to pronounce that Sentence : The Complaint is now ſo generally againſt all *Husbands,* that it giveth great ſuſpicion of its being often ill-grounded; it is impoſſible they ſhould all deſerve that Cenſure, and therefore it is certain,

tain, that it is many times misapplyed : he that *spareth* in every thing is an *inexcusable Niggard,* he that *spareth* in nothing is as *inexcusable a Madman*; the *mean* is, to spare in what is least neceffary, to lay out more liberally in what is most required in our several citcumstances; yet this will not always satisfie, there are *Wives* who are impatient of the Rules of Oeconomy, and are apt to call their *Husbands* Kindness in question, if any other meafure is put to their expence than that of their own Fancy; be sure to avoid this dangerous Errour, such a partiality to your Self, which is so offensive to an understanding Man, that he will very ill bear a *Wife's* giving her self such an injurious *preference* to all the *Family,* and whatever belongeth to it : But to admit the worst, and that your *Husband* is really a *Close-handed Wretch,* you must in this, as in other Cases, endeavour to make it less afflicting to you; and first you must observe *seasonable hours of speaking.*

When you offer any thing in opposition to this reigning Humour, a *third hand* and a *wise Friend,* may often prevail more than you will be allowed to do in your own Cause: Sometimes you are dextrously to go along with him in things, where you see that the niggardly part of his Mind

is

is moſt predominant, by which
you will have the better opportunity of perſwading him
in things where he may be
more indifferent : Our *Paſſions* are very unequal, and are
apt to be raiſed or leſſened,
according as they work upon
different Objects ; they are
not to be *ſtopped* or *reſtrained*
in thoſe things where our
Mind is more particularly engaged : In other matters they
are more tractable, and will
ſometimes give Reaſon a hear-
ing, and admit a fair Diſpute.
More than that, there are few
Men, even in this inſtance of
Avarice, ſo intirely abandoned
to it, that at ſome hours, and
upon ſome occaſions, will not
forget their natures, and for

that

that time turn Prodigal ; the same Man who will *grudge* himfelf what is *neceffary*, let his *Pride* be raifed and he fhall be *profufe* ; at another time his *Anger* fhall have the fame effect ; a fit of *Vanity*, *Ambition*, and fometimes of *Kindnefs*, fhall open and inlarge his *narrow Mind* ; a Dofe of Wine will work upon this tough humour, and for the time diffolve it : Your bufinefs muft be, if this Cafe happeneth, to watch thefe *critical moments*, and not let one of them flip without making your advantage of it ; and a *Wife* may be faid to want skill, if by thefe means fhe is not able to fecure her felf in a good meafure againft the Inconveniencies this

fcurvy

scurvy quality in a *Husband*
might bring upon her, ex-
cept he should be such an incurable Monster, as I hope
will never fall to your
share.

The last supposition I will
make, is, That your *Husband*
should be *weak* and *incompe-
tent* to make use of the Privi-
leges that belong to him ; it
will be yielded, that such a
one leaveth room for a great
many Objections ; but God
Almighty seldom sendeth a
Grievance without a *Remedy*,
or at least such a Mitigation as
taketh away a great part of
the sting, and smart of it. To
make such a *Misfortune* less
heavy, you are first to bring
to your Observation, That a

D 5 *Wife*

Wife very often maketh the better Figure, for her *Huf-bands* making no great one, and there feemeth to be little reafon, why the fame *Lady* that chufeth a *Waiting-Woman* with *worfe Looks*, may not be content with a *Husband* with *lefs Wit*; the Argument being equal from the advantage of the Comparifon : If you will be more afhamed in fome Cafes, of fuch a *Husband*, you will be lefs afraid than you would perhaps be of a wife one ; his *Unfeafonable Weak-nefs* may no doubt fometimes grieve you, but then fet a-gainft this, that it giveth you the *Dominion*, if you will make the right ufe of it ; it is next to his being dead, in which

which Cafe the *Wife* hath right
to Adminifter ; therefore be
fure, if you have fuch an Ide-
ot, that none, except your
felf, may have the benefit of
the forfeiture : Such a Fool is
a dangerous Beaft, if others
have the keeping of him ; and
you muft be very undextrous
if when your *Husband* fhall
refolve to be an *Afs*, you do
not take care he may be *your
Afs* ; but you muft go skillfully about it, and above all
things, take heed of diftinguifhing in publick what kind
of *Husband* he is ; your inward thoughts muft not hin-
der the outward payment of
the confideration that is due
to him ; your *flighting* him in
Company , befides that, it
would,

would, to a difcerning By-ftan-
der, give too great encouragement for the making near-
er application to you, is in
it felf fuch an undecent way
of affuming, that it may provoke the tame Creature to
break loofe, and to fhew his
Dominion for his Credit, which
he was content to forget for
his Eafe : In fhort, the fureft
and the moft approved me-
thod will be to do like a wife
Minifter to an eafie *Prince* ;
firft give him the Orders
you afterwards receive from
him ; with all this, that which
you are to pray for, is a *Wife*
Husband, one that by know-
ing how to be a *Mafter,* for
that very reafon will not let
you feel the weight of it ; one
whofe

whose Authority is so soften'd
by his Kindness, that it giveth you ease without abridg-
ing your *Liberty* ; one that
will return so much tender-
ness for *Juft Efteem* of him,
that you will never want *pow-*
er, though you will seldom
care to use it ; such a *Huf-*
band is as much above all the
other Kinds of them, as a
rational fubjection to a Prince,
great in himself, is to be preferr'd before the difquiet and
uneasiness of *Unlimited Li-*
berty.

Before I leave this Head, I
muft add a little concerning
your *Behaviour* to your *Huf-*
bands Friends, which requireth the moft refined part of
your Underftanding to ac-
quit

quit your felf well of it; you
are to ftudy how to live with
them with more care than you
are to apply to any other part
of your Life; efpecially at
firft, that you may not ftum-
ble at the firft fetting out; the
Family into which you are
grafted will generally be apt
to expeƈt, that like a Stran-
ger in a Foreign Country, you
fhould conform to their Methods, and not bring in a new
Model by your own Authority; the *Friends* in fuch a Cafe
are tempted to rife up in
Arms as againft an unlawful
Invafion, fo that you are
with the utmoft Caution to
avoid the leaft Appearances of
any thing of this kind; and
that you may with lefs difficulty

culty afterwards give your Directions, be sure at first to receive them from your *Hus-bands* Friends, gain them to you by early applying to them, and they will be so satisfied, that as nothing is more thankful than Pride, when it is complyed with, they will strive which of them shall most recommend you; and when they have helped you to take Root in your *Husband's* good Opinion, you will have less dependance upon theirs, though you must not neglect any reasonable means of preserving it.

You are to consider, that a Man govern'd by his *Friends,* is very easily inflamed by them; and that one who is
not

not fo, will yet for his own fake expect to have them confider'd. It is eafily improved to a point of honour in a *Husband,* not to have his *Relations* neglected; and nothing is more dangerous, than to raife an Objection, which is grounded upon *Pride*; it is the moft ftubborn and lafting Paffion we are fubject to, and when it is the firft caufe of the *War,* it is very hard to make a fecure *Peace* : your *Caution* in this is of the laft importance to you; and that you may the better fucceed in it, carry a ftrict Eye upon the *Impertinencies* of your *Servants* ; take heed that their ill *humour* may not engage you to take Exceptions, or their

too

too much affuming in fmall
matters, raife Confequences
which may bring you under
great difadvantage.

Remember that in the cafe
of a *Royal Bride*, thofe about
her are generally fo far fu-
fpected to bring in a Foreign
Intereft, that in moft Coun-
tries, they are infenfibly redu-
ced to a very fmall number,
and thofe of fo low a Figure,
that it doth not admit the being *Jealous* of them. In little,
and in the Proportion, this
may be the Cafe of every *New-
Married-Woman*, and therefore it may be more advife-
able for you, to *gain the Servants* you find in a Family,
than to tye your felf too faft
to thofe you carry into it; you
are

are not to overlook thofe
fmall Reflections, becaufe they
may appear low and inconfi-
derable; for it may be faid,
that as the *greateft ftreams* are
made up of the *fmall drops* at
the head of the Springs from
whence they are derived, fo
the *greateft circumftances* of
your Life, will be in fome degree directed by thefe *feeming
trifles*, which having the advantage of being the firft acts
of it, have a greater effect than
fingly in their own nature
they could pretend to.

I will conclude this Article
with my Advice, that you
would, as much as Nature will
give you leave, endeavour to
forget the great *Indulgence*
you have found at home, after
fuch

such a gentle Difcipline as you have been under; every thing you diflike will feem the harfher to you, the tendernefs we had for you, *My Dear*, is of another nature, peculiar to kind Parents, and differing from that you will meet with at firft in any Family into which you fhall be tranfplanted; and yet they may be very kind too, and afford no juftifiable reafon to you to complain. You muft not be frighted with the firft Appearances of a *differing Scene*; for when you are ufed to it, you may like the Houfe you go to, better than that you left; and your *Husband's* Kindnefs will have fo much advantage of ours, that we

fhall

fhall yield up all *Competition*, and as well as we love you, be very well contented to Surrender to fuch a *Rival.*

HOUSE, FAMILY, and CHILDREN.

YOU muft lay before you, *My Dear*; there are degrees of Care to recommend your felf to the World in the feveral parts of your Life, in many things, though the doing of them well, may raife your *Credit* and *Efteem*, yet the omiffion of them would draw no immediate reproach upon you; in others, where your duty is more particularly applyed, the *neglect* of them is amongft thofe Faults which are

not

not forgiven, and will bring you under a *Cenfure*, which will be much a heavier thing than the trouble you would avoid; of this kind is the *Government* of your *Houfe, Family* and *Children*, which fince it is the Province allotted to your Sex, and that the *difcharging it well*, will for that reafon be expected from you, if you either defert it out of *Lazinefs*, or manage it with *want of skill*, inftead of a *help* you will be an *Incumbrance* to the *Family* where you are placed. I muft tell you, that no *refpect* is lafting, but that which is produced by our being in fome degree ufeful to thofe that pay it : where that faileth, the Homage and the Reverence

verence go along with it, and
fly to others where something
may be expected in exchange
for them; and upon this prin-
ciple the *respects* even of the
Children and the *Servants* will
not stay with one that doth
not think them worth their
Care, and the old *House-keeper*
shall make a better Figure in
the Family, than the *Lady*
with all her fine Cloths, if she
wilfully relinquish her Title
to the *Government*; therefore
take heed of carrying your
good Breeding to such a height,
as to be good for nothing, and
to be proud of it : some think
it hath a great Air to be a-
bove troubling their thoughts
with such ordinary things as
their *House* and *Family*; o-
thers

thers dare not admit *Cares* for fear they fhould haften *Wrinkles* ; miftaken *Pride* maketh fome think they muft keep themfelves up, and not defcend to thofe Duties, which do not feem enough refined for great *Ladies* to be imploy'd in ; forgetting all this while, that it is more than the greateft *Princes* can do, at once to preferve refpect, and to neglect their bufinefs ; no *Age* ever erected *Altars* to *infignificant Gods* ; they had all fome quality applyed to them to draw *worfhip* from *Mankind* ; this maketh it the more unreafonable for a *Lady* to expect to be confider'd, and at the fame time refolve not to deferve it ; *good looks* alone will

will not do, they are not
such a lasting *Tenure*, as to be
relyed upon; and if they
should stay longer than they
usually do, it will by no
means be safe to. depend
upon them; for when time
hath abated the violence of
the first liking, and that the
Napp is a little worn off,
though still a good degree of
kindness may remain, Men
recover their sight which before might be dazell'd, and
allow themselves to object as
well as admire; in such a
Case, when a *Husband* seeth
an empty airy thing that
fails up and down the House
to no purpose, and looks as
if she came thither only to
make a Visit, when he findeth,

eth, that after her *Emptiness* hath been extream busy about some very senseless thing, that she eats her Breakfast half an hour before Dinner, to be at greater liberty to afflict the Company with her Discourse; then calleth for her Coach, that she may trouble her Acquaintance, who are already cloy'd with her : And having some *proper Dialogues* ready to display her *Foolish Eloquence* at the top of the Stairs, she setteth out like a Ship out of Harbour, laden with trifles, and cometh back with them ; at her return she repeateth to her faithful Waiting-Woman, the *Triumphs* of that day's *Impertinence,* then wrap'd up in Flattery and clean Linen,

E

nen, goeth to Bed fo fatisfied, that it throweth her into pleafant Dreams of her own Felicity ; fuch a one is feldom ferious but with her *Taylor* ; her *Children* and *Family* may now and then have a random thought, but fhe never taketh aim but at fomething very Impertinent.

I fay when a *Husband*, whofe Province is without Doors, and to whom the Oeconomy of the Houfe would be in fome degree Indecent, findeth no *Order* nor *Quiet* in his *Family*, meeteth with *Complaints* of all kinds fpringing from this Root, the *Miftaken Lady*, who thinketh to make *amends* for all this, by having a well-chofen *Petty-Coat*, will at laft be convinvinced of her *Error*, and with grief be forced to undergo the Penalties that belong to thofe who are wilfully *Infignificant* ; when this fcurvy hour cometh upon her, fhe firft groweth Angry ; then when the time of it is paft, would perhaps grow wifer, not remembring that we can no more have Wifdom than Grace, when ever we think fit to call for it ; there are Times and Periods fix'd for both ; and when they are too long neglected, the Punifhment is, that they are *Irrecoverable*, and nothing remaineth but an ufelefs *Grief* for the Folly of having thrown them out of our Power ; you are to think what a mean Figure

a Woa Woman maketh, when she is so degraded by her own Fault; whereas there is nothing in those Duties which are expected from you, that can be a lessening to you, except your want of *Conduct* make it so.: You may love your *Children* without living in the *Nursery*, and you may have a *competent* and *discreet care* of them, without letting it break out upon the Company, or exposing your self by turning your Discourse that way, which is a kind of *Laying Children* to the *Parish*, and it can hardly be done any where, that those who hear it will be so forgiving, as not to think they are overcharged with them. A Wo-mans

mans *tenderneſs* of her *Children* is one of the leaſt de-
ceitful Evidences of her Vertue ; but yet the way of ex-
preſſing it, muſt be ſubjeƈt to
the Rules of *good Breeding:*
And though a *Woman* of *Quality* ought not to be leſs kind
to them, than *Mothers* of the
meaneſt Rank are to theirs,
yet ſhe may diſtinguiſh her
ſelf in the *manner,* and avoid
the courſe Methods, which in
Women of a lower ſize
might be more excuſable.
You muſt begin early to
make them *Love* you, that
they may *Obey* you: This
Mixture is no where more
neceſſary than in Children ;
and I muſt tell you, that you
are not to expeƈt Returns of

Kind-

Kindneſs from yours, if ever you have any, without Grains of Allowance; and yet it is not ſo much a *defect* in their *good Nature*, as a *ſhortneſs of Thought* in them; Their firſt *Inſufficiency* maketh them lean ſo entirely upon their *Parents* for what is *neceſſary*, that the *habit* of it maketh them continue the ſame *Expectations* for what is *unreaſonable*; and as oft as they are *denied*, ſo often they think they are *injured*; and whilſt their *Deſires* are ſtrong, and their *Reaſons* yet in the Cradle, their *Anger* looketh no farther than the thing they long for and cannot have; and to be *diſpleaſed* for their *own good*, is a

Maxim

Maxim they are very flow to underftand ; fo that you may conclude, the firft Thoughts of your *Children* will have no fmall Mixture of Mutiny ; which being fo natural, you muft not be angry, except you would increafe it ; you muft deny them as feldom as you can, and when there is no avoiding it, you muft do it *gently,* you muft flatter away their ill Humours, and take the next Opportunity of pleafing them in fome other things, before they either ask or look for it : This will ftrengthen your *Authority,* by making it foft to them ; and confirm their *Obedience,* by making it their Intereft.

E 4　　　　You

You are to have as strict a Guard upon your self amongst your *Children*, as if you were amongst your *Enemies*; they are apt to make wrong Inferences, to take Encouragement from half Words, and misapplying what you may say or do, so as either to lessen their *Duty*, or to extend their *Liberty* farther than is convenient : Let them be more in awe of your *Kindness* than of your *Power*, and above all, take heed of supporting a *Favourite Child* in its Impertinence, which will give Right to the rest of claiming the same Privilege. If you have a divided Number, leave the *Boys* to the *Fathers* more peculiar Care,

Care, that you may with the greater Juſtice pretend to a more immediate Juriſdiction over thoſe of your own *Sex :* You are to live ſo with them, that they may never chuſe to avoid you, except when they have *offended* ; and then let them tremble, that they may diſtinguiſh ; But their Penance muſt not continue ſo long as to grow *ſowre* upon their *Sto-machs*, that it may not *har-den* in ſtead of *correcting* them : The kind and ſevere Parts muſt have their ſeveral *turns* ſeaſonably applied ; but your *Indulgence* muſt have the broader mixture, that *Love*, rather than *Fear*, may be the Root of their *Obedi-ence*.

E 5　　　　Your

Your *Servants* are in the next place to be confidered; and you muft remember not to fall into the miftake of thinking, That becaufe they receive Wages, and are fo much *Inferiour* to you, therefore they are *below* your Care to know how to mannage them. It would be as good Reafon for a *Mafter Workman* to defpife the *Wheels* of his *Engine* becaufe they are made of *Wood.* Thefe are the *Wheels* of your *Family*; and let your Directions be never fo faultlefs, yet if thefe *Engines* ftop or move wrong, the whole Order of your *Houfe* is either at a ftand, or difcompofed: Befides, the *Inequality* which is between you,

you, muſt not cauſe you to forget, that *Nature* maketh no ſuch diſtinction, but that *Servants* may be looked upon as *humble Friends*, and that *Returns* of *Kindneſs* and *good Uſage* are as much due to ſuch of them as deſerve it, as their *Service* is due to *us* when we require it. A *fooliſh haughtineſs* in the Style of *ſpeaking*, or in the manner of *commanding* them, is in it ſelf very undecent, beſides, that it begetteth an *Averſion* in them, of which the leaſt ill Effect to be expected, is, that they will be *ſlow* and *careleſs* in all that is injoyned them, and you will find it true by your Experience, that you will be ſo much the more

obeyed

obeyed as you are lefs *Imperious.* Be not *too hafty* in giving your *Orders,* nor *too angry* when they are not altogether *obferved*; much lefs are you to be loud, or too much difturbed; an *evennefs* in diftinguifhing when they do *well* or *ill,* is that which will make your *Family* move by a Rule, and without Noife, and will the better fet out your Skill in conducting it with Eafe and Silence, that it may be like a well-difciplin'd Army, which knoweth how to anticipate the Orders that are fit to be given them. You are never to neglect the Duty of the *prefent Hour,* to do another thing, which though it may be better in

it

it felf, is not to be un-
feafonably preferred. Allot
well chofen Hours for the
Infpection of your *Fami-
ly*, which may be fo diftin-
guifhed from the reft of your
Time, that the *neceffary Cares*
may come in their proper
Places, without any Influ-
ence upon your good Hu-
mour, or Interruption to o-
ther things. By thefe Me-
thods you will put your felf
'in poffeffion of being valued
by your Servants, and then
their *Obedience* will naturally
follow.

I muft not forget one of
the greateft *Articles* belonging to a *Family*, which is the
Expence: It muft not be fuch, as
by failing either in the Time
or

or meaſure of it, may rather draw *Cenſure* than gain *Applauſe.* If it was well Examined, there is more Money given to be laughed at, than for any other thing in the World, though the Purchaſers do not think ſo. A wellſtated Rule is like the *Line,* when that is once paſs'd we are under another *Pole*; ſo the firſt *ſtraying* from a *Rule,* is a ſtep towards making that which was before a *Vertue,* to change its Nature, and to grow either into a *Vice,* or at leaſt an *Impertinence :* The Art of laying out Money wiſely, is not attained to without a great deal of thought; and it is yet more difficult in the Caſe of
a *Wife,*

a *Wife,* who is accountable to her *Husband* for her miſtakes in it : It is not only his *Money,* his *Credit* too is at Stake, if what lyeth under the *Wife's* Care is managed, either with undecent *Thrift,* or too looſe *Profuſion* ; you are therefore to keep the *Mean* between theſe two *Extreams,* and it being hardly poſſible to hold the Balance exactly even, let it rather incline towards the *Liberal* ſide, as more ſuitable to your *Quality,* and leſs ſub-ject to *Reproach* ; of the two, a little *Money* miſpent is ſoon-er *recovered,* than the *Credit* which is loſt by having it un-handſomely *ſaved* ; and a Wiſe *Husband* will leſs for-give a ſhameful piece of *Par-ſimony,*

simony, than a little *Extravagance,* if it is not too often repeated; his *Mind* in this muſt be your chief *Direction;* and his *Temper,* when once known, will in a great meaſure juſtifie your part in the management, if he is pleaſed with it.

In your *Cloths* avoid too much Gaudineſs; do not value your ſelf upon an *Imbroidered-Gown;* and remember, that a *reaſonable Word,* or an *obliging Look,* will gain you more reſpect, than all your *fine Trappings.* This is not ſaid to reſtrain you from a *decent Compliance* with the World, provided you take the wiſer, and not the fooliſher part of your Sex for
your

your Pattern: Some *distincti-
ons* are to be allowed, whilst
they are well-suited to your
Quality and *Fortune*, and in
the distribution of the Expence, it seemeth to me, that
a *full Attendance*, and *well-cho-
sen Ornaments* for your House,
will make you a better Figure, than *too much glittering*
in what you wear, which may
with more ease be imitated
by those which are below
you; yet this must not tempt
you to starve every thing but
your own Apartment; or in
order to more abundance
there, give just cause to the
least Servant you have, to
complain of the want of what
is necessary: Above all, fix it
in your thoughts, as an unchangeable

changeable *Maxim,* That nothing is *truly fine* but what is
fit, and that juft fo much as
is proper for your *Circum-*
ftances of their feveral kinds,
is much finer than all you can
add to it; when you once
break through thofe bounds,
you launch into a wide Sea of
Extravagance, every thing will
become neceffary, becaufe you
have a mind to it; and you
have a mind to it, not becaufe
it is *fit* for you, but becaufe
fome body elfe *hath it :* This
Lady's Logick fetteth *Reafon*
upon its Head, by carrying
the *Rule* from *things* to *Per-*
fons, and appealing from what
is *right* to every Fool that is
in the *wrong;* the word *necef-*
fary is miferably applyed, it
difor-

diſordereth *Families*, and o-
verturneth *Governments* by being ſo abuſed : Remember, that
Children and *Fools* want every thing, becauſe they want
Wit to diſtinguiſh : and therefore there is not a ſtronger
Evidence of a *Crazy Under-*
ſtanding, than the making too
large a Catalogue of things
neceſſary, when in truth there
are ſo very few things that
have a right to be placed in
it ; try every thing firſt in
your *Judgement*, before you
allow it a place in your *De-*
ſire, elſe your *Husband* may
think it as neceſſary for him
to deny, as it is for you to
have whatever is unreaſonable ; and if you ſhall too often give him that advantage,
the

the habit of *refufing* may per-haps reach to things that are not unfit for you ; there are unthinking *Ladies*, who do not enough confider, how lit-tle their own Figure agreeth with the *fine things* they are fo proud of ; others when they have them, will hardly allow them to be *vifible* ; they cannot be feen without *Light*, and that is many times fo fawcy and fo prying, that is like a too forward *Gallant* to be for-bid the *Chamber* to. Some, when you are uſhered into their *Dark Ruelle*, it is with fuch fo-lemnity, that a Man would fwear there was fomething in it, till the *Unskilful Lady* breaketh fi-lence, and beginneth a Chat, which difcovereth it is Puppit-Play

Play with Magnificent Scenes; many esteem things rather as they are hard to be gotten, than that they are worth getting : This looketh as if they had an Interest to pursue that Maxim, because a great part of their own *value* dependeth upon it. Truth in these Cases would be very often *unmannerly*, and might derogate from the *Prerogative*, great *Ladies* would assume to themselves, of being distinct Creatures from those of their Sex, who are inferiour, and of less difficult access in other things too. Your Condition must give the rule to you, and therefore it is not a Wifes part to aim at more than a bounded *Liberality* ; the farther extent

of

of that *Quality* (otherwife to be commended) belongeth to the *Husband,* who hath better means for it.

Generofity wrong placed becometh a *Vice,* and it is no more a *Vertue* when it groweth into an *Inconvenience.* *Vertues* muft be inlarged or reftrained according to the differing Circumftances ; A *Princely Mind* will undo a *private Family,* therefore things muft be fuited, or elfe they will not deferve to be Commended, let them in themfelves be never fo valuable ; and the Expectations of the World are beft anfwered when we acquit our felves in that manner which feemeth to be prefcribed to our feveral Condi-

Conditions, without ufurping upon thofe Duties, which do not fo particularly belong to us.

I will clofe the confideration of this *Article* of *Expence*, with this fhort word, Do not *fetter* your felf with fuch a *Reftraint* in it as may make you *Remarkable* ; but remember that *Vertue* is the greateft *Ornament*, and good *Sence* the *beft Equipage*.

BEHAVIOUR and CONVERSATION.

IT is time now to lead you out of your *Houfe* into the *World*. A Dángerous ftep ; where your Vertue alone will not ferve you, except it is attended

tended with a great deal of *Prudence* : You muſt have *both* for your *Guard*, and not ſtir without them; the Enemy is abroad, and you are ſure to be taken, if you are found ſtragling: Your *Behaviour* is therefore to incline ſtrongly towards the *Reſerved part* : your *Character* is immovably to be fixed upon that Bottom, not excluding a mixture of greater freedom, as far as it may be innocent and well-timed. The *Extravagancies* of the Age have made *Caution* more neceſſary ; and by the ſame reaſon that the too great Licence of Ill Men hath by Conſequence in many things reſtrained the Lawful Liberty of thoſe who did not

not abuſe it, the unjuſtifiable
Freedom of ſome of your
Sex have involved the reſt in
the Penalty of being redu-
ced. And though this can-
not ſo alter the Nature of
things, as to make that *Criminal*, which in it ſelf is *Indifferent* ; yet if it maketh it,
dangerous, that alone is inſuffi-
cient to juſtifie the *Reſtraint*.
A *cloſe behaviour* is the fitteſt
to receive *Vertue* for its con-
ſtant *Gueſt*, becauſe there, and
there only, it can be ſecure.
Proper *Reſerves* are the Out-
works, and muſt never be de-
ſerted by thoſe who intend to
keep the Place ; they keep
off the poſſibility not only of
being *taken*, but of being *at-
tempted* ; and if a Woman
F   ſeeth

feeth Danger at never fo remote a Diftance, fhe is for that time to fhorten her *Line of Liberty:* She who will allow her felf to go to the *utmoft Extents* of every thing that is *Lawful*, is fo very near going farther, that thofe who lie at watch, will begin to count upon her.

Mankind, from the double temptation of *Vanity* and *Defire*, is apt to turn every thing a *Woman* doth to the *hopeful fide*; and there are few who dare make an impudent Application, till they difcern fomething which they are willing to take for an *Encouragement:* It is fafer therefore to prevent fuch *Forwardnefs*, than to go about to *cure* it : It gathereth
Strength

Strength by the firſt *allowances*, and claimeth a Right from having been at any time ſuf- fered with Impunity : Therefore nothing is with more care to be avoided, than ſuch a kind of *Civility* as may be miſtaken for *Invitation*. It will not be enough for you to keep your ſelf free from any criminal *Engagements* ; for if you do that which either raiſeth *Hopes*, or createth *Diſcourſe*, there is a Spot thrown upon your Good Name ; and thoſe kind of Stains are the harder to be taken out, being dropped upon you by the *Man's Vanity*, as well as by the *Woman's Malice*. Moſt Men are in one ſence *Platonick Lovers*, though they are not willing to own that *Character*; they are so far *Philosophers*, as to allow, that the greatest part of Pleasure lieth in the *Mind*; and in pursuance of that *Maxim*, there are few who do not place the Felicity more in the Opinion of the World, of their being *prosperous Lovers*, than in the *Blessing* it self, how much soever they appear to value it. This being so, you must be very cautious not to gratifie those *Camelions* at the price of bringing a *Cloud* upon your *Reputation*, which may be deeply wounded, though your *Conscience* is unconcerned. Your own Sex too will not fail to help the least Appearance

pearance that giveth a *Handle* to be ill turned ; the beſt of them will not be diſpleaſed to improve their own Value, by laying others under a *Diſadvantage*, when there is a fair Occaſion given for it ; It diſtinguiſheth them ſtill the more, their own *Credit* is ſtill the more exalted, and, like a Picture ſet off with Shades, ſhineth more when a *Lady*, leſs *Innocent*, or leſs *Diſcreet*, is ſet near, to make them appear ſo much the brighter. If theſe lend their Breath to blaſt ſuch as are ſo unwary as to give them this Advantage, you may be ſure there will be a ſtronger Gale from thoſe, who, beſides *Malice* or *Emulation*, have

an

an *Intereſt* too, to ſtrike hard
upon a Vertuous Woman:
It ſeemeth to them, that their
Load of Infamy is leſſened,
by throwing part of it upon
others; ſo that they will not
only improve when it lieth
in their way, but take pains
to find out the leaſt miſtake
an *Innocent Woman* commit-
teth, in Revenge of the In-
jury ſhe doth in leading a
Life which is a Reproach to
them. With theſe you muſt
be extream *wary,* and neither
provoke them to be *angry,*
nor invite them to be *inti-
mate.*

To the *Men* you are to
have a *Behaviour* which may
ſecure you, without offend-
ing them: No ill-bred affe-
ęted

ted *Shineſs* nor *Roughneſs*, unſuitable to your *Sex*, and unneceſſary to your *Vertue* ; but a way of Living that may prevent all courſe *Railleries* or *unmannerly Freedoms* ; *Looks* that forbid without *Rudeneſs*, and oblige without *Invitation*, or leaving room for the ſawcy Inferences Mens Vanity ſuggeſteth to them upon the leaſt Encouragements. This is ſo very nice, that it muſt engage you to have a perpetual *Watch* upon your *Eyes*, and to remember, that one careleſs *Glaunce* giveth more advantage than a *hundred Words* not enough conſidered ; the *Language* of the *Eyes* being very much the moſt *ſignificant*, and the moſt

F. 4. *obſerved.*

obſerved. Your *Civility*, which is always to be preſerved, muſt not be carried to a *Compliance*, which may betray you into irrecoverable Miſtakes. This *French* ambiguous word *Complaiſance* hath led your Sex into more blame, than all other things put together : It carrieth them by degrees into a certain thing called a *good kind* of *Woman*, an eaſie *Idle Creature*, that doth neither *Good* nor *Ill* but by *chance*, hath no *Choice*, but leaveth that to the Company ſhe keepeth. *Time*, which by degrees addeth to the ſignification of *Words*, hath made her , according to Modern Stile, little better than one who thinketh it a *Rudeneſs*

to

to deny, when civilly required, either her *Service in Per-*
fon, or her *friendly Affiftance,*
to thofe who would have a
meeting, or want a *Confident.*
She is a certain thing always
at hand, an eafie *Companion,*
who hath ever great *Compaffion*
for *diftreffed Lovers :* She cen-
fureth nothing but *Rigour,*
and is never without a *Plaifter*
for a *wounded Reputation,* in
which chiefly lieth her Skill
in *Chirurgery :* She feldom
hath the Propriety of any
particular Gallant, but liveth
upon *Brokage,* and waiteth
for the Scraps her Friends are
content to leave her.

There is another *Character*
not quite fo *Criminal,* yet not
lefs *Ridiculous ;* which is that

of

of a *good-humour'd Woman,*
one who thinketh she must
always be in a *Laugh,* or a
broad *Smile* ; and because
Good-Humour is an obliging
Quality, thinketh it less ill-
manners to talk *impertinently,*
than to be silent in Company.
When such a prating *Engine*
rideth *Admiral,* and carrieth
the *Lanthorn* in a *Circle of
Fools,* a *cheerful Coxcomb* com-
ing in for a *Recruit,* the *Chat-
tering* of *Monkeys* is a better
noise than such a *Concert* of
sencelefs Merriment : If she is
applauded in it, she is so en-
couraged, that, like a *Bal-
lad singer,* who, if commended, breaketh his Lungs, she
letteth her self loose, and o-
verfloweth upon the Company.

ny. She conceiveth that
Mirth is to have no Intermiſ-
ſion, and therefore ſhe will
carry it about with her,
though it be to a *Funeral*;
and if a Man ſhould put a
familiar Queſtion, ſhe doth
not know very well how to
be angry, for then ſhe would
be no more that pretty thing
called a *Good humour'd Woman*. This neceſſity of appea-
ring at all times to be infinite-
ly pleaſed, is a grievous miſtake; ſince in a *handſom Woman* that *Invitation* is unneceſſary; and in one who is
not ſo, *ridiculous*.

It is not intended by this,
that you ſhould forſwear
Laughing; but remember, that
Fools being always painted
in

in that posture it may fright
those who are wise from doing it too frequently, and going too near a Copy which is
so little inviting, and much
more from doing it *loud*, which
is an unnatural Sound, and
looketh so much like ano-
ther Sex, that few things are
more offensive. That *boi-*
strous kind of *Jollity* is as
contrary to *Wit* and *Good*
manners, as it is to *Modesty*
and *Vertue* ; besides, it is a
course kind of quality, that
throweth a Woman into a
lower Form, and degradeth
her from the Rank of those
who are more refined. Some
Ladies speak *aloud* and make
a *noise* to be the more mind-
ed, which looketh as if they
beat

beat their *Drums* for *Volun-
tiers* , and if by misfortune
none come in to them, they
may, not without reason, be
a good deal out of Counte-
nance.

There is yet one thing
more to be avoided, which
is the *Example* of those who
intend nothing farther than
the Vanity of *Conquest*, and
think themselves secure of not
having their Honour tainted
by it. Some are apt to believe their *Vertue* is too *Ob-
scure*, and not *enough known*,
except it is exposed to a
broader Light, and set out to
its best advantage, by some
publick Trials; these are dangerous Experiments, and generally fail, being built upon

on so weak a foundation, as
that of too great *Confidence* in
our selves; it is as safe to play
with *Fire*, as to dally with
Gallantry.

Love is a Paffion that hath
Friends in the Garrifon, and
for that reafon muft by a
Woman be kept at fuch a diftance, that fhe may not be
within the danger of doing
the moft ufual thing in the
World, which is confpiring
againft her Self, elfe the humble Gallant, who is only admitted as a Trophy, very often becometh the Conquerour;
he putteth on the ftyle of Victory, and from an *Admirer*
groweth into a *Mafter*, for fo
he may be called from the
moment he is in Poffeffion.
The

The firſt Reſolutions of ſtopping at good Opinion and Eſteem, grow weaker by degrees againſt the Charms of *Courtſhip* skillfully applyed. A Lady is apt to think a Man ſpeaketh ſo much reaſon whilſt he is *Commending* her, that ſhe hath much ado to believe him in the wrong when he is making Love to her, and when beſides the natural Inducements your Sex hath to be merciful, ſhe is bribed by well-choſen *Flattery*, the poor Creature is in danger of being caught like a Bird liſtening to the Whiſtle of one that hath a Snare for it. *Conqueſt* is ſo tempting a thing, that it often maketh Women miſtake Mens *Submiſſions;* which with

all

all their fair Appearances, have generally lefs *Refpect* than *Art* in them. You are to remember, that Men who fay extream fine things, many times fay them moft for their own fakes, and that the vain Gallant is often as well pleafed with his own *Compliments*, as he could be with the *kindeft anfwer*; where there is not that *Oftentation* you are to fufpect there is a *Defign*; and as ftrong *perfumes* are feldom ufed but when they are neceffary to fmother an unwelcome *fcent*; fo *Excefs* of *good Words*, leave room to believe they are ftrewed to cover fomething which is to gain admittance under a Difguife : You muft be therefore upon your Guard, and

and confider, that of the two,
Refpect is more dangerous
than *Anger*, it puts even the
beft Underftandings out of
their place, till the time of
their fecond thoughts reftore
them ; it ftealeth upon us infenfibly, throweth down our
Defences, and maketh it too
late to refift, after we have
given it that advantage ,
whereas railing goeth away
in found , it hath fo much
noife in it, that by giving
warning it befpeaketh Caution. *Refpect* is a flow and fure
Poifon, and like *Poifon* fwelleth us within our felves ,
where it prevaileth too much,
it groweth to be a kind of
Apoplexia in the Mind, turneth it quite round, and after
it

it hath once feized the underftanding, becometh *mortal* to
it : For thefe reafons, the fafeft way is to treat it like a
fly Enemy, and be perpetu-
ally upon the watch againft
it.

I will add one *Advice* to
conclude this head, which is,
that you will let every feven
years make fome alteration in
you towards the *Graves* fide,
and not be like the *Girls* of
Fifty, who refolve to be always *Young*, what ever *Time*
with his Iron Teeth hath de-
termined to the contrary ; unnatural things carry a *Deformity* in them never to the *Dif-
guifed* ; the *Livelinefs* of *Youth*
in a riper Age, looketh like
an *old patch* upon a *new Gown* ;
fo

ſo that a *Gay Matron*, a chearful *old Fool* may be reaſonably put into the Liſt of the *Tamer* kind of *Monſters:* There is a certain Creature call'd a *Grave Hobby-Horſe*, a kind of ſhe *Numps*, that pretendeth to be pulled to a Play, and muſt needs go to *Bartholomew-Fair*, to look after the young Folks, of whom ſhe onely ſeemeth to take care, when in reality ſhe onely taketh them for her excuſe; ſuch an old *Butterfly* is of all *Creatures* the moſt ridiculous, and the ſooneſt found out. It is good to be early in your Caution, to avoid any thing that cometh within diſtance of ſuch deſpicable Patterns, and not like ſome *Ladies*, who

defer

defer their *Converſion*, till they have been ſo long in poſſeſſion of being laughed at, that the World doth not know how to change their ſtyle, even when they are re-claimed from that which gave the firſt occaſion for it ; the advantages of being *reſerved* are too many to be ſet down, I will only ſay, that it is a *Guard* to a *good Woman*, and a *Diſguiſe* to an *ill one*. It is of ſo much uſe to both, that thoſe ought to uſe it as an *Ar-tifice*, who refuſe to practiſe it as a *Vertue*.

FRIEND.

FRIENDSHIPS.

I Muſt in a particular manner recommend to you a
ſtrict Care in the Choice of
your *Friends* ; perhaps the
beſt are not without their
Objections, but however, be
ſure that yours may not ſtray
from the Rules which the wiſer part of the World hath ſet
to them ; the Leagues *Offen-
ſive* and *Defenſive,* ſeldom hold
in *Politicks,* and much leſs is
Friendſhips ; the violent *Inti-
macies,* when once broken, of
which they ſcarce ever fail,
make ſuch a *Noiſe,* the Bag of
Secrets

Secrets untied, they fly about like Birds let loose from a Cage, and become the *Entertainment* of the *Town*. Besides, these great *Dearnesses* by degrees grow *injurious* to the rest of your *Acquaintance*, and throw them off from you: There is such an *Offensive* Distinction when the *Dear Friend* cometh into the Room, that it is *flinging Stones* at the *Company*, who are not apt to forgive it.

Do not lay out your *Friendship* too *lavishly* at first, since it will, like other things, be so much the sooner spent; neither let it be of too quick a *growth*; for as the Plants which shoot up too *fast* are not of that *continuance*, as those thofe which take more time for it ; fo too fwift a Progrefs in pouring out your *Kindnefs,* is a certain Sign that by the Courfe of Nature it will not be *long-lived.* You will be refponfible to the World, if you pitch upon fuch *Friends* as at the fame time are under the weight of any *Criminal Objection* ; in that cafe you will bring your felf under the difadvantages of their *Character,* and muft bear your part of it. *Chufing* implieth *Approving* ; and if you fix upon a *Lady* for your *Friend* againft whom the World fhall have given Judgment, 'tis not fo well natur'd as to believe you are altogether *averfe* to her way of *living,* fince

since it doth not discourage
you from admitting her into
your *Kindness* ; and *Resemblance* of *Inclinations* being
thought none of the least
Inducements to *Friendship*,
you will be looked upon at
least as a well-wisher if not a
Partner with her in her Faults:
If you can forgive them in another, it may be presumed you
will not be less gentle to your
self ; and therefore you must
not take it ill, if you are reck-
oned a *Croupiere*, and con-
demned to pay an equal Share
with such a friend of the *Reputation* she hath lost.

If it hapneth that your
Friend should fall from the
State of *Innocence* after your
Kindness was engaged to her,
you

you may be flow in your be-
lief in the beginning of the
Difcovery ; but as foon as
you are convinced by a *Ra-*
tional Evidence , you muft ,
without breaking too *roughly,*
make a fair and quick *Retreat*
from fuch a *Miftaken Acquain-*
tance ; elfe by moving *too*
flowly from one that is fo
tainted, the Contagion may
reach you fo far as to give you
part of the *Scandal*, though
not of the *Guilt.* This Matter is fo nice, that as you muft
not be too hafty to *joyn* in
the *Cenfure* upon your *Friend*
when fhe is *accufed*, fo you
are not on the other fide to
defend her with too much
warmth ; for if fhe fhould
happen to deferve the Re-

port of *Common Fame*, befides
the Vexation that belongeth
to fuch a miftake, you will
draw an *ill appearance* upon
your felf, and it will be
thought you pleaded for her
not without fome *confideration* of your felf. The *Anger*
which muft be put on to vin-
dicate the *Reputation* of an
injured Friend, may incline
the Company to fufpect you
would not be fo *zealous*, if
there was not a poffibility
that the Cafe might be your
own: For this reafon you are
not to carry your *dearnefs* fo
far, as abfolutely to lofe your
Sight where your Friend is
concerned: Becaufe *Malice* is
too quick-fighted, it doth not
follow, that *Friendfhip* muft be
blind :

blind: There is to be a *Mean* between those *Extreams*, else your Excuse of Good Nature may betray you into a very *ridiculous Figure*, and by degrees may be preferr'd to such Offices as you will not be proud of. Your *Ignorance* may lessen the *Guilt*, but will improve the *Jest.* upon you, who shall be kindly sollicitous to procure a Meeting, and innocently contribute to the *Ills* you would avoid ; whilst the *Contriving Lovers*, when they are alone, shall make you the Subject of their *Mirth*, and perhaps (with respect to the Goddess of *Love* be it spoken) it is not the worst part of their *Entertainment*, at least it is the

G 2 most

moſt laſting, to laugh at the *believing Friend*, who was ſo eaſily deluded.

Let the good Senſe of your *Friends* be a chief Ingredient in your *Choice* of them ; elſe let your *Reputation* be never ſo clear, it may be clouded by their *Impertinence.* It is like our Houſes being in the Power of a Drunken and Careleſs Neighbour ; only ſo much worſe, as that there will be no *Inſurance* here to make you amends, as there is in the Caſe of Fire.

To conclude this Paragraph ; If *Formality* is to be allowed in any Inſtance, it is to be put on to reſiſt the Intruſion of ſuch forward Women as ſhall preſs themſelves into

into your *Friendſhip,* where,
if admitted, they will be either a *Snare* or an *Incumbrance.*

CENSURE.

IT will come next to your
Conſideration, how you
are to mannage your *Cenſure* ;
in which both Care and Skill
will be a good deal required,
to diſtinguiſh is not only *natural* but *neceſſary* ; and the
Effect of it is, That we cannot avoid giving Judgment
in our Minds, either to *ab-
ſolve* or to *condemn* as the Caſe
requireth. The *Difficulty* is,

to know where and when it is proper to *proclaim* the *Sentence.* An *Averfion* to what is *Criminal,* and a *Contempt* of what is *ridiculous,* are the *infeparable Companions* of Underftanding and Vertue ; but the letting them go farther than our own Thoughts, hath fo much danger in it, that though it is neither poffible nor fit to *fupprefs* them intirely, yet it is neceffary they fhould be kept under great *Reftraints.* An *unlimited Liberty* of this kind is little lefs than fending a *Herald* to proclaim War to the World, which is an *angry Beaft* when fo provoked : The Conteft will be *unequal,* though you are never fo much in the right ; and if you begin

gin againſt ſuch an Adverſa-
ry, it will tear you in pieces,
and with this Juſtification,
That it is done in its own
defence. You muſt therefore
take heed of *Laughing*, except in Company that is very
ſure ; it is throwing Snow-
balls againſt Bullets ; and it
is the *diſadvantage* of a Woman, that the Malice of the
World will help the Brutality
of thoſe who will throw a
ſlovenly Untruth upon her.
You are for this Reaſon to
ſuppreſs your *Impatience* ; for
Fools, (which beſides that they
are too ſtrong a Party to be
unneceſſarily provoked) are,
and of all other the moſt dangerous. In this Caſe, a *Block-
head* in his *Rage* will return

a *dull Jest*, which will lie heavy, though there is not a *Grain* of *Wit* in it. Others will do it with more Art, and you muſt not think your ſelf ſecure becauſe your *Reputation* may perhaps be out of reach of *Ill-will* ; for if it findeth that part *guarded*, it will ſeek one which is more *expoſed* ; it flieth, like a corrupt Humour in the Body, to the *weakeſt* Part : If you have a *tender Side*, the World will be ſure to find it, and to put the worſt *Colour* on all you ſay or do, give an *Aggravation* to every thing that may leſſen you, and a *ſpiteful turn* to every thing that might recommend you. *Anger* laieth open thoſe Defeẟs which *Friend-*

Friendſhip would not ſee, and *Civility* would be willing to forget. *Malice* needeth no ſuch *Invitation* to encourage it, neither are any *Pains* more ſuperfluous than thoſe we take to be ill ſpoken of. If *Envy*, which never dyeth, and ſeldom ſleepeth, is content ſometimes to be in a *Slumber*, it is very unſkilful to make a noiſe to *awaken* it : Beſides, your *Wit* will be miſapplied in it, if it is wholly directed to diſcern the *Faults* of *others*, when it is ſo neceſſary to be ſo often uſed to *mend* and *prevent your own*. The ſending our Thoughts too much abroad, hath the ſame Effect, as when a *Family* never ſtayeth at home ; *Neglect* and *Diſ-*

G 5 *order*

order naturally followeth; as it muſt do within our ſelves, if we do not frequently turn our Eyes inwards, to ſee what is amiſs with us, where it is a ſign we have an *unwelcome Proſpeĉt*, when we do not care to *look* upon it, but rather ſeek our *Conſolations* in the *Faults* of thoſe we converſe with. Avoid being the firſt in fixing a *hard Cenſure*, but let it be confirmed by the *general Voice*, before you give credit to it: Neither are you then to give Sentence like a *Magiſtrate*, or as if you had a *ſpecial Authority* to beſtow a *good* or *ill Name* at your diſcretion. Do not dwell too long upon a *weak Side*, touch and go away;

way; take pleasure to stay longer where you can commend, like Bees that fix only upon those Herbs out of which they may extract the Juice of which their Honey is composed. A *Vertue* stuck with *Bristles* is too rough for this Age; it must be adorned with some *Flowers*, or else it will be unwillingly entertained; so that even where it may be fit to strike, do it like a *Lady*, gently; and assure your self, that where you take care to do it, you will wound others more, and hurt your self less, by *soft Strokes*, than by being *harsh* or *violent*. The Triumph of *Wit* is to make your *good Nature* subdue your *Censure*; to be quick

in

in *seeing Faults*, and flow in *exposing* them. You are to consider, that the invisible thing called a *Good Name*, is made up of the Breath of Numbers that speak well of you; so that if by a *disobliging Word* you silence the *meanest*, the *Gale* will be less strong which is to bear up your *Esteem.* And though nothing is so vain as the eager pursuit of *empty Applause*, yet to be well thought of, and to be kindly used by the World, is like a *Glory* about a Womans *Head*; 'tis a Perfume she carrieth about with her, and leaveth where-ever she goeth; 'tis a Charm against *Ill-will*; *Malice* may empty her Quiver, but cannot wound;

the

the Dirt will not ſtick, the
Jeſts will not take : Without
the conſent of the World, a
Scandal doth not go deep ; it
is only a ſlight ſtroke upon
the Party injured, and return-
eth with the greater force upon thoſe that gave it.

VANITY and AFFEC-TATION.

I Muſt with more than ordinary *earneſtneſs* give you
Caution againſt *Vanity*, it being the Fault to which your
Sex ſeemeth to be the moſt
inclined , and ſince *Affectation*
for the moſt part attendeth
it , I do not know how to
divide

divide them : I will not call them *Twins* , becaufe more properly *Vanity* is the *Mother*, and *Affectation* the Darling Daughter : *Vanity* is the Sin, and *Affectation* the Punifh-ment ; the firft may be called the Root of *Self-Love*, the o-ther the *Fruit* ; *Vanity* is ne-ver at its full growth till it fpreadeth into *Affectation*, and then it is compleat. Not to dwell any longer upon the de-finition of them, I will pafs to the means and motives to a-void them: In order to it, you are to confider, that the World challengeth the right of diftributing Efteem and Ap-plaufe; fo that where any af-fume by their fingle *Authority*, to be their own *Carvers* ; it

groweth

groweth angry, and never faileth to seek *Revenge*; and if we may meafure a Fault by the greatnefs of the *Penalty*, there are few of a higher fize than *Vanity*, as there is fcarce a Punifhment which can be heavier than that of being laughed at. *Vanity* maketh a Woman tainted with it, fo top-ful of her felf, that fhe fpilleth it upon the *Company*; and becaufe her own thoughts are intirely imployed in *Self-Contemplation*; fhe endeavoureth, by a cruel Miftake, to confine her *Acquaintance* to the fame narrow Circle of that which only concerneth her Ladifhip, forgetting that fhe is not of half that *Importance* to the World, that fhe

she is to her self, so mistaken
she is in her Value, by being
her own Appraiser; she will
fetch such a Compass in Discourse to bring in her beloved
Self, and rather than fail, her
fine Petty-Coat, that there
can hardly be a better Scene
than such a Tryal of ridiculous Ingenuity: It is a Pleasure
to see her Angle for *Commendation,* and rise so dissatisfied
with the Ill-bred *Company,* if
they will not *bite.* To observe
her throwing her *Eyes* about
to fetch in Prisoners, and go
about Cruizing like a Pri-
vateer, and so out of *Counte-
nance,* if she return without
Booty, is no ill piece of Co-
medy: She is so eager to draw
respect, that she always mis-
seth

ſeth it, yet thinketh it ſo much
her due, that when ſhe faileth ſhe groweth *waſpiſh*, not
conſidering, that it is impoſſible to commit a Rape upon
the will. That it muſt be
fairly gained, and will not be
taken by *Storm* ; and that in
this Caſe, the Tax ever ri-
ſeth higheſt by a *Benevolence.*
If the World inſtead of ad-
miring her *Imaginary Excel-
lencies*, taketh the Liberty to
laugh at them, ſhe *appealeth*
from it to her ſelf, for whom
ſhe giveth *Sentence*, and pro-
claimeth it in all *Companies* :
On the other ſide, if incoura-
ged by a *Civil Word*, ſhe is ſo
obliging, that ſhe will give
thanks for being laughed at in
good Language : She taketh
a *Com-*

a *Complement* for a Demonstration, and setteth it up as an *Evidence*, even against her Looking-Glass; but the good *Lady* being all this while in a most profound *Ignorance* of her self, forgetteth that Men would not let her talk upon them, and throw so many *fenceless words* at their heads, if they did not intend to put her Person to Fine and Ransome for her *Impertinence.* Good words of any other Lady, are so many Stones thrown at her, she can by no means bear them, they make her so uneasie, that she cannot keep her *Seat*; but up she riseth, and goeth home half burst with *Anger* and *Strait-Lacing*; if by great chance she saith any

any thing that hath fence in
it, fhe expecteth fuch an Ex-
ceffive rate of *Commendations*,
that to her thinking the Company ever rifeth in her *Debt* ;
fhe looketh upon *Rules* as
things made for the common
People, and not for Perfons
of her *Rank* ; and this Opinion fometimes provokes her to
Extend her Prerogative to the
difpencing with the Com-
mandments : If by great *For-*
tune fhe happeneth, in fpite of
her *Vanity*, to be honeft, fhe
is fo troublefome with it, that
as far as in her lieth, fhe maketh a *fcurvy* thing of it ; her
bragging of her *Vertue*, looketh as if it coft her fo much
pains to get the better of her
Self, that the *Inferences* are
very

very ridiculous. Her *good Hu-mour* is generally applied to the laughing at *good Sence.* It would do one good to fee how heartily fhe defpifeth any thing that is fit for her to do. The greateft part of her *Fancy* is laid out in chufing her *Gown*, as her *Difcretion* is chiefly imploy'd in *not paying* for it. She is faithful to the *Fafhion*, to which not only her *Opinion*, but her *Senfes* are wholly refigned; fo obfequious fhe is to it, that fhe would be ready to be reconciled even to *Vertue* with all its *Faults*, if fhe had her Dancing-Mafter's Word that it was practis'd at Court,

To a Woman fo compos'd, when *Affectation* commeth in
to

to improve her *Character*, it is then raifed to the higheft *Perfection*. She firft fetteth up for a *Fine thing*, and for that Reafon will diftinguifh her felf, right or wrong, in every thing fhe doth. She would have it thought that fhe is made of fo much the *finer Clay*, and fo much more *fifted* than ordinary, that fhe hath no *common Earth* about her: To this end fhe muft neither move nor fpeak like other Women, becaufe it would be *vulgar*; and therefore muft have a Language of her *own*, fince *ordinary Englifh* is too courfe for her. The *Looking-glafs* in the Morning dicta-teth to her all the *Motions* of the Day, which by how much

the

the more *studied*, are so much
the more *mistaken*. She cometh into a Room as if her
Limbs were set on with ill-
made Screws, which maketh
the Company fear the pretty
thing should leave some of
its *artificial Person* upon the
Floor. She doth not like
her self as *God Almighty* made
her, but will have some of
her own Workmanship; which
is so far from making her a
better thing than a *Woman*,
that it turneth her into a
worse Creature than a *Mon-
key*. She falleth out with
Nature, against which she maketh War without admitting
of a *Truce*, those Moments ex-
cepted in which her *Gallant*
may reconcile her to it, when
she

she hath a mind to be *soft*
and *languishing*: There is
something so unnatural in
that *affected Easiness*, that her
Frowns could not be by many degrees so forbidding.
When she would appear un-
reasonably *humble*, one may
see she is so excessively *proud*,
that there is no enduring it.
There is such an *impertinent
Smile*, such a *satisfied Simper*,
when she faintly disowneth
some fulsom Commendation a
Man hapneth to bestow upon
her against his Conscience,
that her *Thanks* for it are
more visible under such a
thin *Disguise*, than they could
be if she should *print* them.
If a *handsomer Woman* taketh
any liberty of *Dressing* out
of

of the ordinary Rules, the miſtaken Lady followeth, without diſtinguiſhing the *unequal Pattern*, and maketh her ſelf *uglier* by an Example miſplaced ; either forgetting the Privilege of *good Looks* in *another*, or preſuming, without ſufficient reaſon, upon *her own*. Her *Diſcourſe* is a *ſenſleſs Chime* of *empty Words*, a heap of *Complements* ſo equally applied to differing *Perſons*, that they are neither valu'd nor believ'd. Her *Eyes* keep pace with her *Tongue*, and are therefore always in *motion* ; one may diſcern that they generally incline to the *compaſſionate* ſide, and that, notwithſtanding her pretence to *Vertue*, ſhe is gentle to *diſtreſſed*

ftreffed Lovers , and *Ladies*
that are *merciful*. She will
repeat the tender part of a
Play fo feelingly , that the
Company may guefs, without
Injuftice; fhe was not altogether a *difintereffed Spectator*.
She thinketh that *Paint* and
Sin are concealed by railing at them; upon the latter
fhe is lefs hard, and being
divided between the two op-
pofite Prides of her *Beauty*
and her *Vertue*, fhe is often
tempted to give broad Hints
that fome body is dying for
her; and of the two fhe is
lefs unwilling to let the
World think fhe may be
fometimes profan'd, than that
fhe is never worfhipped. Very great *Beauty* may perhaps
H

fo dazle for a time, that Men may not fo clearly fee the *De-formity* of thofe *Affections*: But when the *Brightnefs* goeth off, and that the *Lover's Eyes* are by that means-fet at liberty to fee things as they are, he will naturally return to his loft Senfes, and recover the Miftake into which the Lady's *good Looks* had at firft engaged him; and being once undeceived, ceafeth to worfhip that as a *Goddefs*, which he feeth is only an *artificial Shrine*, moved by *Wheels* and *Springs* to delude him. Such Women pleafe only like the *firft Opening* of a *Scene*, that hath nothing to recommend it but the being *New*: They may be compared to *Flies*,

that

that have pretty shining *Wings* for two or three hot Months, but the first cold Weather maketh an end of them; so the *latter Season* of these *fluttering Creatures* is dismal: From their nearest Friends they receive a very faint Respect; from the rest of the World, the utmost degree of Contempt.

Let this *Picture* supply the place of any other *Rules* which might be given to prevent your *resemblance* to it. The *Deformity* of it, well considered, is *Instruction* enough, from the very same reason, that the sight of a *Drunkard* is a better *Sermon* against that *Vice*, than the best that was ever preach'd upon that *Subject*. H 2 PRIDE.

PRIDE.

AFter having said this
against *Vanity*, I do not
intend to apply the same *Censure* to *Pride*, well placed,
and rightly defined. It is an
ambiguous Word ; one kind
of it is as much a *Vertue*, as
the other is a *Vice :* But we
are naturally so apt to chuse
the *worst*, that it is become
dangerous to commend the
best side of it. A Woman
is not to be proud of her
fine Gown ; nor when she
hath less Wit than her Neigh-
bours, to comfort her self
that

that she hath more Lace.
Some Ladies put so much
weight upon *Ornaments*, that
if one could see into their
Hearts, it would be found,
that even the Thoughts of
Death are made less heavy to
them by the Contemplation
of their being *laid out* in *State*,
and *honourably attended* to the
Grave. One may come a
good deal short of such an
Extream, and yet still be sufficiently *Impertinent*, by set-
ting a wrong Value upon
things which ought to be
used with more indifference.
A Lady must not appear sollicitous to ingross *Respect* to
her self, but be content with
a reasonable *Distribution*, and
allow it to others, that she

may have it returned to her. She is not to be troublesomly *nice*, nor diftinguifh her felf by being too *delicate*, as if ordinary things were too *courfe* for her; this is an *unmannerly* and *offenfive* Pride, and where it is practifed, deferveth to be mortified, of which it feldom faileth. She is not to lean too much upon her Quality, much lefs to defpife thofe who are below it. Some make *Quality* an *Idol*, and then their *Reafon* muft fall down and worfhip it; they would have the World think, that no amends can ever be made for the want of a *great Title*, or ancient *Coat of Arms:* They imagine, that with thefe *Advantages* they

ftand

ſtand upon the *higher Ground,* which maketh them look down upon *Merit* and *Vertue,* as things inferiour to them. This Miſtake is not only *ſenceleſs,* but *criminal* too, in putting a greater Price upon that which is a piece of *good Luck,* than upon things which are valuable in themſelves. *Laughing* is not enough for ſuch a *Folly;* it muſt be ſeverely *whipped,* as it juſtly deſerves. It will be confeſſed, there are frequent *Temptations* given by *pert Upſtarts* to be angry, and by that to have our Judgment corrupted in theſe Caſes; but they are to be reſiſted, and the utmoſt that is to be allowed, is, when thoſe of a *new Edition* will for-

forget themselves, so as either
to brag of their *weak side*, or
to endeavour to hide their
Meanness by their *Insolence*;
to cure them by a little seasonable *Raillery*, a little
Sharpness well placed, without dwelling too long upon
it. These and many other
kinds of *Pride* are to be a-
voided. That which is to
be recommended to you, is,
an *Emulation* to raise your self
to a *Character*, by which you
may be distinguished, an Ea-
gerness for precedence in
Vertue, and all such other
things as may gain you a greater share in the good Opinion
of the World. *Esteem* to *Vertue* is like a *cherishing Air* to
Plants and *Flowers*, which
maketh

maketh them blow and prof-
per; and for that reafon it
may be allowed to be in fome
degree the *Caufe* as well as the
Reward of it. That *Pride*
which leadeth to a *good End*,
cannot be a *Vice*, fince it is
the beginning of a *Vertue*; and
to be pleafed with juft *Ap-
plaufe*, is fo far from being a
Fault, that it would be an
ill Symptom in a Woman, who
fhould not place the greateft
part of her *Satisfaction* in it.
Humility is no doubt a great
Vertue; but it ceafeth to be fo,
when it is afraid to fcorn an
ill thing. Againft *Vice* and
Folly it is becoming your *Sex*
to be *haughty*; but you muft
not carry the *Contempt* of
things to *Arrogance* towards
Perfon

Perſons, and it muſt be done with fitting *Diſtinctions,* elſe it may be *Inconvenient* by being unſeaſonable. A *Pride* that raiſeth a little *Anger* to be out-done in any thing that is good, will have ſo good an *Effect,* that it is very hard to allow it to be a Fault. It is no eaſie matter to carry even between theſe differing kinds ſo deſcribed; but remember, that it is ſafer for a *Woman* to be thought too proud, than too familiar.

DIVER-

DIVERSIONS.

THE laſt thing I ſhall recommend to you, is a
wiſe and ſafe method of uſing
Diverſions; to be too eager
in the purſuit of pleaſure
whilſt you are *Young*, is dangerous; to catch at it in riper
Years, is graſping a ſhadow
that will not be held; beſides,
that by being leſs natural it
groweth to be indecent; *Diverſions* are the moſt properly
to be applied, to eaſe and
relieve thoſe who are *Oppreſ-
ſed*, by being too much Imployed; thoſe that are *Idle*
have

have no need of them, and yet they above all others give themfelves up to them. To un-bend our *Thoughts*, when they are too much ftretched by our Cares, is not more natural than it is neceffary, but to turn our whole Life into a *Holy-day*, is not only ridicu-lous, but deftroyeth pleafure inftead of *promoting* it; the *Mind* like the *Body* is tired by being always in one Pofture, too ferious breaketh it, and too diverting loofeneth it : It is *Variety* that giveth the Re-lifh, fo that *Diverfions* too fre-quently reaped, grow firft to be indifferent, and at laft tedious; whilft they are well chofen and well timed, they are never to be blamed; but
when

when they are ufed to an Excefs, though very *Innocent* at
firft, they often grow to be
Criminal, and never fail to
be *Impertinent* : Some Ladies
are befpoken for Merry Meet-
ings, as *Beffus* was for Duels;
they are ingaged in a Circle
of *Idlenefs*, where they turn
round for the whole Year,
without the *Interruption* of a
ferious hour; they know all
the Players Names,& are *Inti-
mately* acquainted with all the
Booths in *Bartholomew Fair*;
no Souldier is more *Obedient*
to the found of his Captain's
Trumpet, than they are to that
which fummoneth them either
to a *Puppit-Play* or a *Monfter*;
the Spring that bringeth out
Flies, and *Fools* maketh them
Inhabitants

Inhabitants in *Hide-Park*; in the Winter they are an Incumbrance to the *Play-Houfe*, and the Ballaft of the *Drawing-Room* ; the Streets all this while are fo weary of thefe daily Faces, that *Mens Eyes* are over-laid with them ; the *fight* is glutted with fine things as the *Stomach* with fweet ones; and when a fair *Lady* will give too much of her felf to the *World*, fhe groweth lufhious, and oppreffeth inftead of pleafing.

Thefe *Jolly Ladies* do fo continually feek *Diverfion*, that in a little time they grow into a *Jeaft*, yet are unwilling to remember, that if they were feldomer feen they would not be fo often *laughed at*; befides,

befides, they make themfelves *Cheap*, than which there cannot be an *unkinder word* beftowed upon your *Sex.* To play fometimes, to entertain *Company*, or to *divert* your felf, is not to be difallowed, but to do it fo often as to be called a *Gamefter*, is to be avoided, next to the things that are moft *Criminal.* It hath Confequences of *feveral kinds* not to be indured ; it will ingage you into a habit of *Idlenefs* and *ill hours*, draw you into ill mixed *Company*, make you neglect your *Civilities* abroad, and your *bufinefs* at home, and impofe into your *Acquaintance* fuch as will do you no Credit. To deep *Play* there will be yet greater *Objections* ; it will give

give *Occasion* to the World to ask *spiteful Questions,* how you dare venture to *lose,* and what means you have to pay such great *sums.* If you pay *exactly,* it will be enquired from whence the *money* cometh ; if you owe, and especially to a Man, you must be so very *Civil* to him for his forbearance, that it layeth a ground of having it farther improved if the *Gentleman* is so disposed, who will be thought no unfair *Creditor,* if where the *Estate* faileth he seizeth upon the Person ; besides, if a *Lady* could see her own Face upon an *ill Game,* at a deep Stake, she would certainly forswear any thing

that

that could put her looks under fuch a *Difadvantage*.

DANCING.

TO *Dance* fometimes will not be imputed to you as a fault, but remember that the end of your *Learning* it, was, that you might know the better how to move *gracefully*; it is only an *advantage* fo far; when it goeth beyond it, one may call it *excelling* in a Miſtake, which is no very great Commendation : It is better for a *Woman* never to *Dance*, becauſe ſhe hath no ſkill in it, than to do it too

I   often,

often, becaufe fhe doth it well; the eafieft as well as the fafeft *Method* of doing it, is in *private Companies*, as a-mongft *particular Friends*, and then carelefly, like a *Diverfion*, rather than with *Solemnity*, as if it was bufinefs, or had any thing in it to deferve a *Months preparation* by ferious Conference with a *Dance-ing-Mafter.*

Much more might be faid to all thefe heads, and many more might be added to them; but I muft reftrain my thoughts, which are full of my Dear Child, and would overflow into a Volume, which would not be fit for a *New-Years-Gift.* I will conclude with my warmeft Wifhes for
all

all that is good to you, that
you may live fo as to be an
Ornament to your Family,and
a Pattern to your Sex, that
you may be bleffed with a
Husband that may value,
and with Children that may
inherit your Vertue; that you
may fhine in the World by a
true Light, and filence Envy
by deferving to be efteemed,
that Wit and Vertue may both
confpire to make you a great
Figure; when they are feparated, the firft is fo empty,
and the other fo faint, that
they fcarce have right to be
commended : May they therefore meet and never part; let
them be your Guardian An-
gels, and be fure never to
ftray out of the diftance of
their

their joint-protection : May you fo raife your Character, that you may help to make the next Age a better thing, and leave Pofterity in your Debt for the advantage it fhall receive by your Example: Let me conjure you, *My Deareft,* to comply with this kind Ambition of a Father, whofe thoughts are fo ingaged in your behalf, that he reckoneth your Happinefs to be the greateft part of his own.

FINIS.